Catch A Kiss

Written by Deborah Diesen ♡ Illustrated by Kris Aro McLeod

In the broad, bright sunlight of the big backyard,
Izzie smiled at her mama. "Mama, blow me a kiss!"

Mama smooched her fingertips.
She blew Izzie a tiny, round kiss. "Here it comes!"

Phoof!

The little kiss landed right on Izzie's nose!

"Another!" cried Izzie.

Mama smooched again.
She blew Izzie a zigzag kiss.
It zipped back and forth.

Zoom.
Zip!

Izzie caught the kiss in the crook of
her elbow. She giggled at the tickly feel.

"Now a triple-decker!" Triple-decker kisses were Izzie's favorite.

Mama smooch-smooch-smooched. She blew once, twice, three times. Three shiny kisses tumbled through the air.

Izzie stretched up and caught the
first one on the tip of her ear.

"Got it!"

Izzie bounced up and caught the
second one on a dimple in her cheek.

"Got it!"

Izzie sprang up for the third one,
the most beautiful of them all.

But she **missed!**

And before she could jump again, a puff of wind grabbed that kiss and pulled it up. High. Higher!

"Oh no!" cried Izzie. "My kiss!"

Izzie ran as fast as she could across the yard.
"I've **got** to catch it!"

She jumped and flapped her arms.
She reached into the wind.

"My kiss!"

She leaped toward the clouds.

Oh, how she wished she could fly!

"I've got to catch that kiss!"

But she couldn't.

Her kiss was gone.

Mama came to Izzie and wrapped her in a soft hug. "Izzie, would you like to know a secret?" asked Mama.

Izzie did not.
She just wanted her kiss back!

But finally, slowly, Izzie nodded.

Mama pointed to a tiny sparkle high
in the sky. Izzie watched as it grew
a little bit bigger,
    and came a little bit closer,
        bit by bit,
        moment by moment,
            until it was right above Izzie.

Mama looked at Izzie. "It's the secret
of kisses," said Mama.

"No matter how far they have to go,
no matter what they have to get through,
and even if they get lost along the way,
Mama-kisses ALWAYS come find you."

And sure enough—

in a shimmery glitter—
Mama's kiss **did**.

SMOOCH!

Izzie hugged her mama and smiled
a big, sunshine smile.

"And I have a secret for **you**," said Izzie.
She launched a kiss of her own into the
bright, wide sky.

"So do mine!"